SHINO
AND THE CHAOS CREW

The Day of the
ESCAPE ROOM OF DOOM

Written by Chris Callaghan

Illustrated by Amit Tayal

Collins

Shinoy and the Chaos Crew

When Shinoy downloads the Chaos Crew app on his phone, a glitch in the system gives him the power to summon his TV heroes into his world.

With the team on board, Shinoy can figure out what dastardly plans the red-eyed S.N.A.I.R., a Super Nasty Artificial Intelligent Robot, has come up with, and save the day.

1 The escape room

Shinoy read the big screen display.

A person's stature is not measured in their size, but in their words.

"How do you measure statues in words?" said Toby. "That doesn't make any sense."

"*Stature*, as in height or status," Myra helped out.

"Not *statue* like in the *Statue* of Liberty," said Mum, doing her best impression of the famous American statue.

"It's just like one of those inspirational quotes that Mr Amitri uses during assemblies," Shinoy groaned. They'd all sat through many of their head teacher's boring lectures.

Toby scratched his head. "Do you think there'll ever be a statue of our head teacher?"

"He's probably working on that right now!"

The screen changed to: "Team Shinoy – Prepare to Enter the Chamber of Doom".

Mum had thought they needed a challenge, so here they were at an escape room. Shinoy and Toby were raring to go.

"Team Shinoy in the Chamber of Doom?" groaned Myra. "I'd rather be doing my homework."

"Don't be such a mini-moaner," said Mum, as she stepped into the room.

"Oh, it's smaller than I was expecting!" said Mum.

"It's a bit whiffy!" said Toby, scrunching up his face.

Shinoy giggled. "Smells like someone's done a massive—"

"That's enough of that," interrupted Mum.

The door slammed shut, sealing them in the bleak, empty room. There were jumbled-up magnetic letters scattered across the wall and a sign.

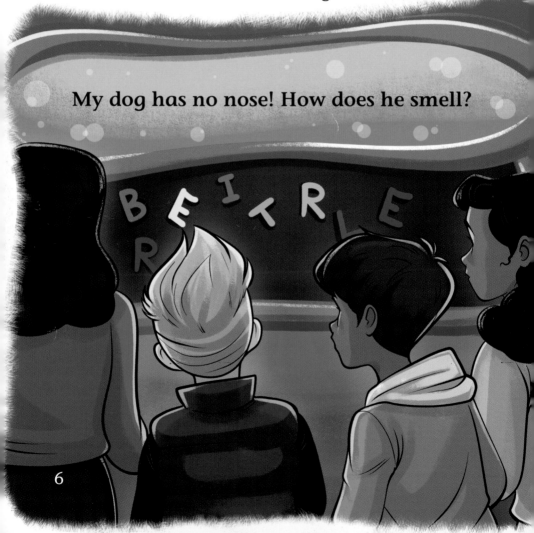

My dog has no nose! How does he smell?

"That's easy," said Shinoy, rearranging the magnetic letters to spell "terrible"!

A hatch popped open, revealing a key.

"That was a little too easy!" said Mum, disappointed.

Shinoy excitedly grabbed the key. "This is going to be epic!"

Myra was still grumbling. "Seriously? Is that all there is to it?"

Shinoy was about to slide the key into a padlock and unlock the door to the next chamber, when another door opened with a whoosh. Above the door was a friendly arrow that flashed and a sign saying: "ENTER". Why was there a key if the next door opened automatically?

Toby bounced through the doorway excitedly and Myra followed. "Let's just get this done and get out of here."

ENTER

But before Mum and Shinoy could enter, the door closed, leaving no sign that it had ever existed. Another, similar door opened with a less friendly sign: "Enter Here or You'll Never See Your Humans Again".

"Well, that's a bit intimidating," said Mum.

Shinoy agreed. It had the bad smell of S.N.A.I.R. about it. "I think we're in big trouble."

They found themselves in a very dark room.

"This is a little more like it," said Mum. "I paid good money for this."

That's odd, thought Shinoy. Mum's voice sounded really far away and squeaky.

A screen flickered into life showing Toby and Myra looking confused. Myra was holding a small box. Then the screen cut to another face, which confirmed Shinoy's fears – S.N.A.I.R. – who snarled: "If you ever want to see your friends, family, pets or whatever they are again, you'll need to navigate the rooms of doom. Or they'll be lost for ever!"

Shinoy already had his hand on his phone before stepping into the room. He could just about hear Mum saying, "I think we need to Call to Action …"

"… Chaos Crew!" finished Shinoy, activating the special app. His voice boomed around the room.

11

The room glowed for a heartbeat, and then there was silence. Shinoy was about to press the app again, but a small voice in the shadows whispered, "What *have* you been up to? You're enormous!"

It was Lazlo. And he wasn't making sense!

In the gloom, Shinoy could just about see the silhouette of the Chaos Crew's stealthiest member moving around. He looked really small.

"How did *you* get in here, Shinoy?" Lazlo asked.

"Through the door," Shinoy said.

Lazlo lit a Tornado Torch. "Well, *this* is the door to this interesting room and *you*, my friend, are too big to fit through it."

Shinoy lifted his head and it crashed on the ceiling. "What's happened to me? How did I get so big?"

"What about *me*? Why am I so tiny?" came a small squeak.

"Mum!" Shinoy laughed. "You're so little!"

"Was it something you ate?" joked Lazlo. "What's that written above the door? 'Your nightmare starts here'! Nice."

Shinoy and Mum explained to Lazlo what had happened, but they couldn't explain how it had happened. How was Shinoy going to get through that door?

"There must be another clue," wondered Lazlo, as he examined the room. "Did you press anything?" They shook their heads. "Or touch anything?" More shaking of heads. "Or say anything?"

Shinoy replayed their conversations over in his head, which was annoyingly brushing against the ceiling.

"Mum said that the first room was *smaller* than she'd expected. Then that the clue had been a *little* easy."

Lazlo raised an eyebrow.

"Then I said that it was going to be *epic* and that we were in *big* trouble."

"Not following you, big man," said Lazlo.

"The sign outside," continued Shinoy. "It said something like 'your stature is not measured in size, but in words'!"

It was weird but did make some kind of sense.

"Make me small, small, small," Shinoy said. He felt a little silly but he noticed that his head wasn't touching the ceiling anymore.

"Make me big, big, big," shouted Mum, as loud as she could.

It worked!

Lazlo watched as Shinoy and Mum made themselves bigger and smaller. They worked out that things changed quicker if they used an assortment of different ways of saying "small" or "big".

Suddenly, the screen burst back into life. "I hate to interrupt," S.N.A.I.R. snarled, "but haven't we forgotten something?"

An image of Myra and Toby briefly appeared. They looked worried.

"At least we're the right size now," Shinoy said, as Lazlo opened the door. Behind it was another very small door. "Or not."

Lazlo handed Shinoy a roll of tape.

"Helio-tape!" Shinoy gasped, recognising it from series 5. Now they'd be able to see in the dark! He tore off short strips and wrapped them around his wrists and ankles. Each strip began to glow brightly. He told Mum to do the same.

3 Ups and downs

"Let's go small!"

miniature   *small*   teeny   tiny

minuscule   mini   wee

weeny   minute   compact   microscopic

shrimp

short   **extra small**

super extra small

mini mini mini!

"Let's go big!"

massive large ginormous

huge big

giant immense

humungous

gigantic

extra large

mammoth

colossal

colossally colossal

super extra large

"Small again!"

miniature minuscule small teeny tiny

weeny minute mini wee microscopic

shrimp short compact extra small

super extra small mini mini mini!

"Big again!"

massive   huge   large   big   ginormous

giant   **gigantic**   humungous   immense

mammoth   colossal   extra large

super extra large   colossally colossal

4 Break out

Finally, they arrived in a small room. There was no obvious exit.

"What do we do now?" asked Mum.

"Enough with the shape-shifting," said Lazlo. "We've got to break free."

Shinoy agreed. "Yeah, let's burst out of here."

They shouted out all the big words they could think of. Soon, they were squashed together and pressing against the walls and ceiling. For a moment, Shinoy wondered if this had been a really bad idea, but then the walls suddenly gave way and they popped out into the most unexpected place imaginable …

… on to the outstretched palm of Myra's hand!

"What were you lot doing in that box?" asked Myra.

Toby's huge eyes loomed closely. "And why are you sooooo little?"

Shinoy explained what had happened. Myra and Toby said they'd been stuck in the dingy room. They'd found a box, which they thought must contain a clue, but they couldn't get it open. The only other thing in the room was a small door with the word "EXIT" above it, which they had ignored, thinking it was a joke.

The light from the Helio-tape was beginning to fade ...

Shinoy, Mum and Lazlo shouted a few well-chosen words until they were the correct size. They burst through the EXIT door and found themselves outside the escape room.

"Check yourselves, people," instructed Lazlo.
"Are we all back to regular dimensions?"

Myra glanced up at Shinoy with
a quizzical look.

"What?" he said defensively.
"I've always been taller than you."

"Not yet, you're not!"

Shinoy smiled and
touched the red
"EXIT" button.
"A bit smaller," he said.

Shinoy returned to
his normal height
and the "EXIT" button
melted into the wall.

"It's a shame we can't keep
changing size," Mum said,
ruffling Shinoy's hair. "I liked it
when you were really small!"

Toby laughed. "Does anyone
want another session? What size
would you like him?"

29

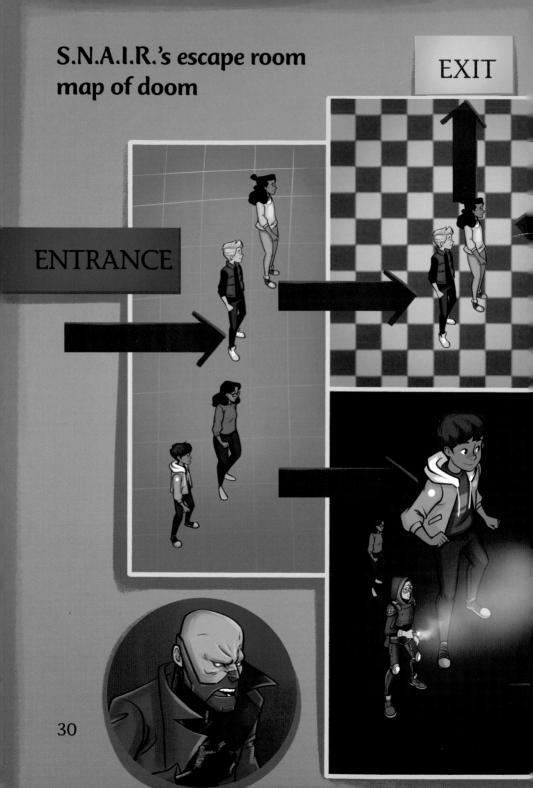

 Ideas for reading

Written by Clare Dowdall, PhD
Lecturer and Primary Literacy Consultant

Reading objectives
- discuss the sequence of events in books and how items of information are related
- discuss and clarify the meanings of words, linking new meanings to known vocabulary
- draw on what they already know or on background information and vocabulary provided by the teacher
- explain and discuss their understanding of books, poems and other material, both those that they listen to and those that they read for themselves.

Spoken language objectives
- use relevant strategies to build their vocabulary
- give well-structured descriptions and explanations

Curriculum links: PSHE – How to cope when things are difficult; English – Vocabulary development

Word count: 1,530

Interest words: inspirational, intimidating, stealthiest, miniscule, minute (as in tiny), mammoth, colossal

Resources: magnetic or cut-out letters, pencils and paper, scissors, internet

Build a context for reading

- Read the title *The Day of the Escape Room of Doom*. Ask children to describe what they know about "escape room" challenges, and what they think an escape room of doom might involve.
- Read the blurb. Invite children to imagine what might make the escape room in the story difficult to escape from.
- Read the interest words. Challenge children to sort them by meaning into two sets (size words and character words). Discuss each word's meaning and ask children to look out for it in the story.

Understand and apply reading strategies

- Read the chapter heading and p3 to the group. Discuss what is happening, to orientate children to the story.